Little Black Ant on Park Street

SMITHSONIAN'S BACKYARD

With lots of love to my son Drew, who constantly finds delight in life's little things.—J.H.

This book is for my mom, Carol Rietz, who loved nature and art. Her love still encourages me.—K.R.

Book copyright © 2009 Trudy Corporation and the Smithsonian Institution, Washington, DC 20560.

Published by Soundprints, an imprint of Trudy Corporation, Norwalk, Connecticut.
www.soundprints.com

Editor: Tracee Williams
Editorial assistance: Anthony Parisi
Book design: Shields & Partners, Westport, CT
Book layout: Katie Sears
Production coordinator: Chris Dobias

First Edition 2009
10 9 8 7 6 5 4 3 2 1 .
Printed in China

Acknowledgments:
    Our very special thanks to Gary Hevel and Natasha Mehdiabadi of the Department of Entomology at the Smithsonian's National Museum of Natural History for their curatorial review of this title.
    Soundprints would also like to thank Ellen Nanney at the Smithsonian Institution's Office of Product Development and Licensing for her help in the creation of this book.

Library of Congress Cataloging-in-Publication Data

Halfmann, Janet.

    Little Black Ant on Park Street / by Janet Halfmann ; illustrated by Kathleen Rietz.—1st ed.
        p. cm.—(Smithsonian's backyard)
    Summary: Follows an ant through her first summer of helping gather food for her nest mates while trying to avoid danger.
    ISBN 978-1-60727-002-7 (hardcover)—ISBN 978-1-60727-004-1 (micro bk.)—ISBN 978-1-60727-003-4 (pbk.)
    1. Ants—Juvenile fiction. [1. Ants—Fiction. 2. Animals—Infancy—Fiction.] I. Rietz, Kathleen, ill. II. Title.
        PZ10.3.H136Lit 2009
        [E]—dc22
                        2008055248

Little Black Ant on Park Street

by Janet Halfmann
Illustrated by Kathleen Rietz

Soundprints
Where Children Discover...

Little Black Ant pokes her head from a tiny sandy hill dotting the lawn of the house on Park Street. It is summertime and the anthill is a flurry of activity.

Beneath the hill lies a busy ant city, with many rooms connected by little tunnels. There are rooms for the ant queens, nurseries for the eggs and babies, a sickroom, food storage rooms and bedrooms for the workers.

For weeks Little Black Ant has worked inside the dark nest under the ground—caring for the queens and young ants, hauling away trash, digging new rooms, and guarding the door to keep out strangers.

Now she is old enough to leave the nest to look for food. She wiggles her antennae, smelling the late afternoon air for danger. All is clear. She scurries up onto the sidewalk.

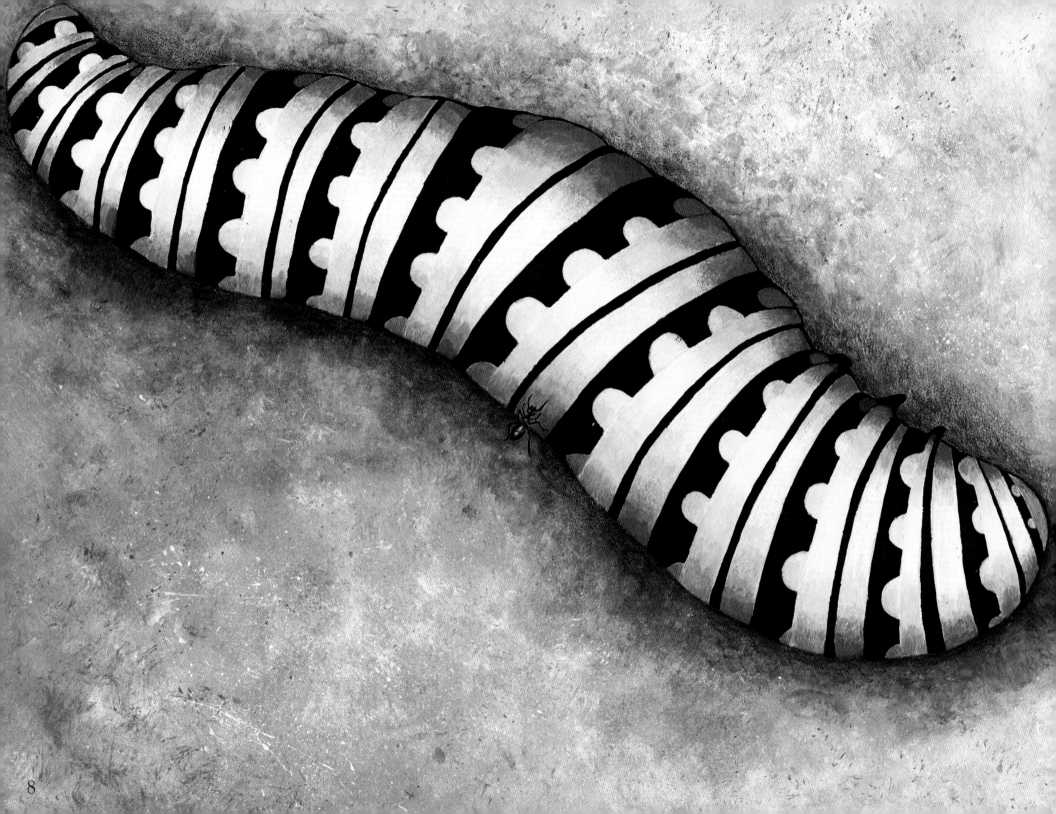

Her antennae wiggle some more, smelling for a whiff
of something tasty. Finally she finds a fat dead caterpillar.
She tries to lift it. She tries to drag it. But it's too heavy.

She runs back to the anthill for help. On the way,
she squirts little drops of liquid from her tail end.
Presto! A scent trail.

Her nest mates pour from the anthill, following the scent trail to the tasty treat. *Chop, chop!* Their sharp jaws slice off bits of caterpillar twenty times heavier than they are. In a slow-moving line, they march back to the nest with their heavy loads.

A summer school class out for a walk
watches the busy two-way ant highway.
The children bend down low to get a closer
look, but are careful not to get in the ants' way.

13

Workers at the nest take the food from Little Black Ant and the others. *Munch, crunch*. They chew the food completely, swallowing the liquid and spitting out the hard parts. The liquid goes into a special "social stomach" for holding food to share.

Then it's dinnertime for everyone! The workers spit up drops of liquid food and feed the queen, babies, and other workers.

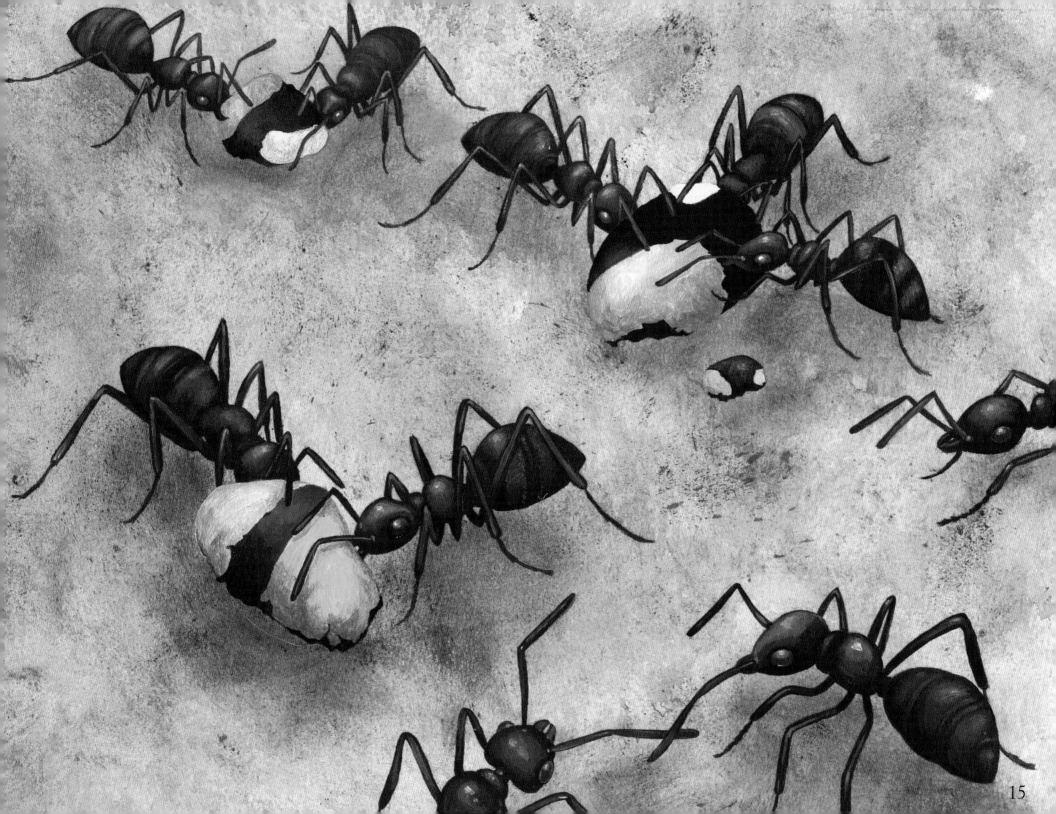

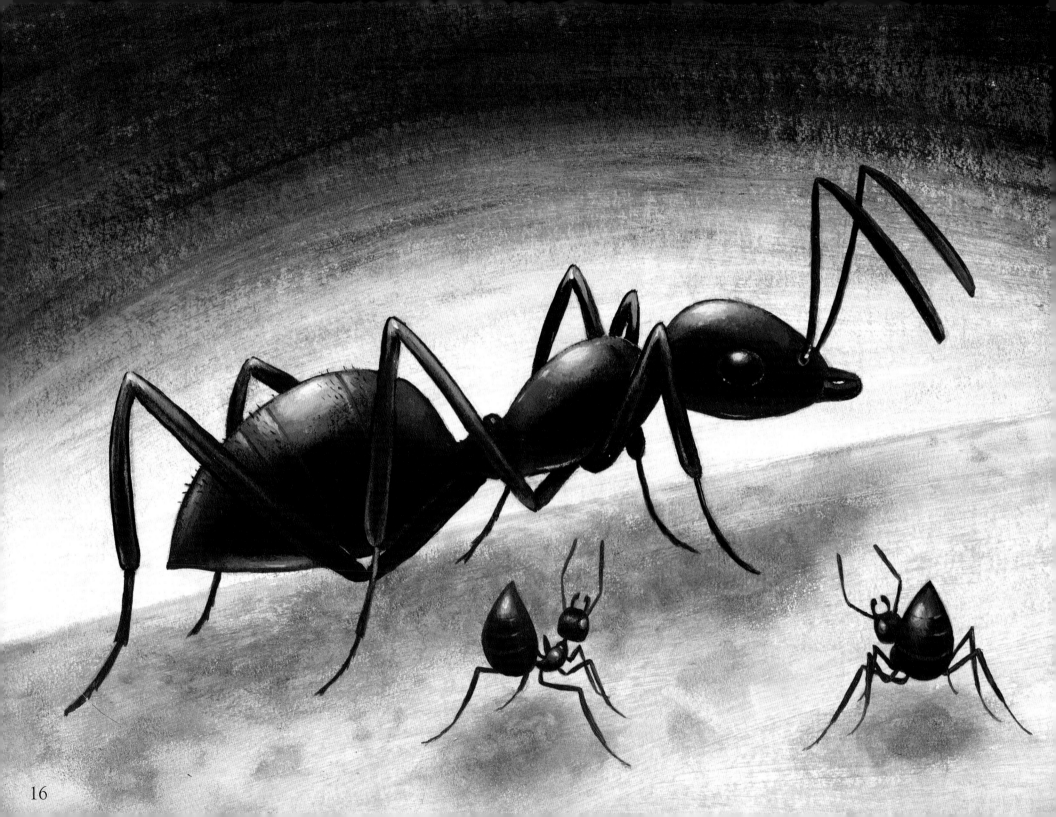

Long after sunset, the ant highway streams on. In the dark, a large carpenter ant tries to steal what's left of the caterpillar. *Whoosh!* Little Black Ant and her nest mates point their stings at the thief, showering her with poison. Sharp jaws latch onto her legs. She limps away, trying to shake her legs free.

The next day, Little Black Ant marches with her nest mates toward a rosebush. Tiny green insects called aphids cling to the bush.

Little Black Ant strokes an aphid with her antennae, and surprise! The aphid releases a sweet drop of liquid sugar called honeydew. Little Black Ant licks it up. She strokes aphid after aphid until her "social stomach" bulges with sweet juice for the queen and babies.

As Little Black Ant runs to the nest, a blue jay lands in her path. Little Black Ant scoots inside a silvery gum wrapper to hide. But soon the wrapper is flying through the air, dangling from the bird's beak. Little Black Ant holds on tight.

Peck, *push*, *peck!* The blue jay tucks the shiny paper into his bulky nest. In a flash, Little Black Ant scrambles from the wrapper and down the rough trunk of the maple tree.

She finds the sidewalk and crawls along its edge. On and on she creeps on her little legs, until stars fill the sky. She wiggles her antennae, but nothing smells like home or her family.

When the sun comes up, she is still scurrying. Around noon, she catches a whiff of something familiar. She stops, wildly waving her antennae.

Tap, tap, tap. Little Black Ant bumps into a line of antennae—and they smell just like her! It's her nest mates, hurrying along a scent trail to a huge neighborhood picnic.

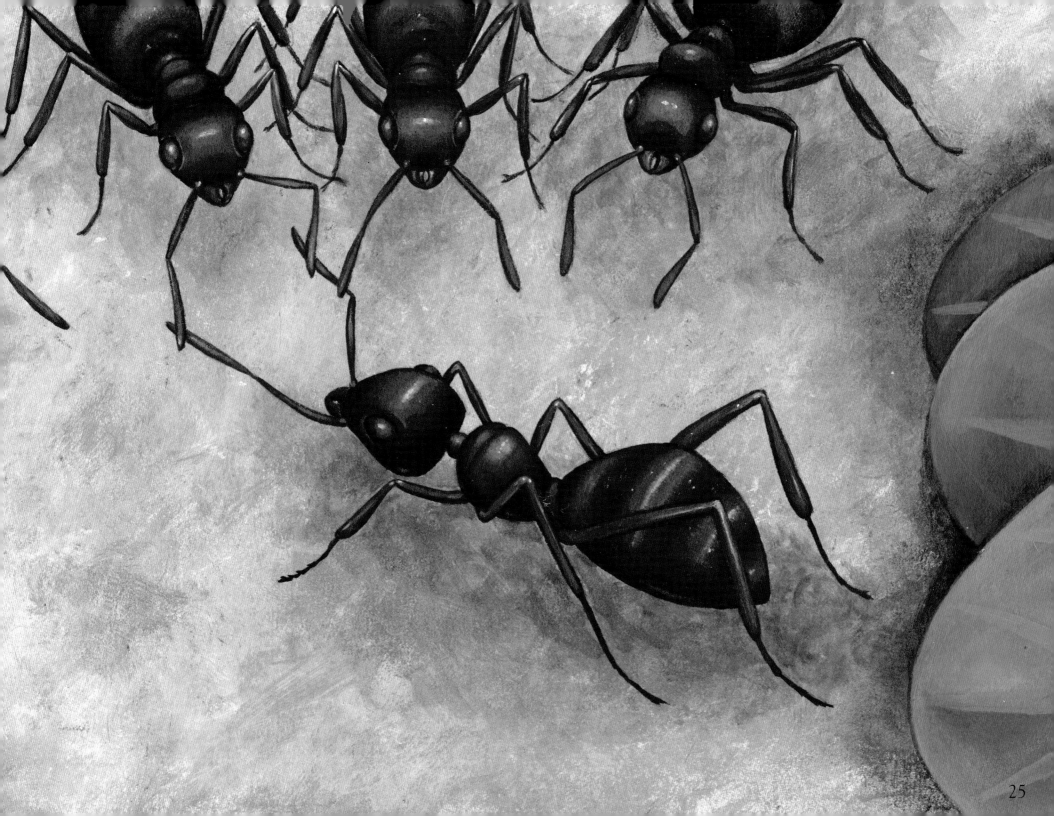

Little Black Ant falls in line and is soon cutting a wedge from a big cookie crumb. All afternoon, she and her nest mates cart bits of food back to the anthill.

As the Park Street picnickers laugh and play in the summer sun, the entire ant city feasts on a picnic of its own!

One warm day toward the end of summer, the anthill buzzes with excitement. Clouds of special ants with silvery wings—males and young queens—fly from the nest. They mate with winged ants from other little black ant colonies.

Their jobs done, the males soon die, and the young queens break off their wings and find places to start new colonies.

As fall winds blow, Little Black Ant helps plug up the entrances to the anthill on Park Street. She and her nest mates crawl to the deepest rooms in the anthill. They huddle together around the queens to sleep away the winter.

Come spring, Little Black Ant will wiggle her antennae once more, searching for cookie crumbs dropped along Park Street.

About the Little Black Ant

The little black ant is native to North America and abundant across the area. It usually builds its nest in soil, with a small dome top above ground. Nests are only a few inches deep, and also may be under stones, logs or the bark of trees.

The little black ant family or colony begins with a young queen. She tends the first batch of eggs alone. The eggs hatch into white worm-like larvae that grow and grow, then become pupae and finally emerge as adult ants.

The first group of ants are all female workers. They search for food and care for future babies and the queen, who now does nothing but lay eggs. All little black ant workers are the same size, about 1/16 of an inch. The queen is twice that size. Colonies can have several queens and thousands of workers.

In the summer, little black ant queens lay eggs that develop into special winged ants—young queens and males. They fly from the nest and mate. The young queens then break off their wings and start new colonies. Queens live about one year and workers about four months.

When a little black ant finds food, it leaves a trail of scent for other workers to follow. Little black ants are active day and night. Outdoors, they eat honeydew and insects that are either alive or dead, helping to keep the earth clean. Sometimes the ants enter houses and form trails to greasy foods and sweets.

Little black ants help control imported red fire ants, major pests with a sting like fire. The native ants compete with the imported ants for nesting places and food and attack the fire ants' colonies. There are about 12,500 known ant species in the world.

Glossary

antennae: two feelers on an ant's head used to sense smell and touch.

ant queens: large female ants who lay all of the eggs for the colony.

aphids: small insects that suck juices from plants for food.

carpenter ant: large ant that nests in wood and is mostly active at night.

colony: large group of ants living together and depending on one another for survival.

honeydew: sweet liquid released by a plant-sucking insect.

social stomach: a special stomach that an ant has in addition to its personal stomach. Also called a crop, it holds food to be shared with the colony.

sting: a small sharp-pointed organ that injects poison.

workers: female ants that do most of the work in the colony.

Points of Interest in this Book